水中的胭脂

Rouge in the Water

张次庚 著

漓江出版社

In Memory of My Father

Alive, you were my first reader …

In heaven you went, riding on the boat of moon and listening to my poetic heart like yesterday …

纪念我的父亲

活着，总是我的第一位读者……

在天堂，正倚着月亮船聆听一颗诗意的心，就像昨天一样……

Dedicated to :

Coral, Lao Dang, and Tannie

给：瑚、老党和坦侬

Acknowledgement

My sincere thanks go to Paul Beech, Cathy DeWolf, Daniel J. Brick, Syed Zaigham S. Jaffery, Omar Eldamsheety, Iain Davie, Lilian Lu, Hailing and the other unlisted friends who have been sharing my poetic heart along the way of my poetry creation.

Thanks for my beloved family that gives me great support for my dream leading to fine poetry.

鸣谢

诚挚地感谢保罗·彼奇、凯茜·德沃芙、丹尼尔·布瑞克、赛义德 .Z.S. 杰菲里、奥尔马·艾尔丹诗提、伊恩·戴维、莉莲、海灵以及未提到的朋友。感谢他们在我的诗歌创作道路上的一路分享。

特别感谢我的家人对我诗歌梦想的支持。

About Author

Cigeng Zhang was educated in Beijing Capital Normal University, majoring in English literature. She is now a freelance English translator. She began posting her English poems on the international website in 2012. Her poems Drunk Smile, What Was Left, Still for You, At 8 O'clock, The Moon, the Poet have been published in the Poetic Bond anthologies in the UK since 2013. Her poems Civet Cat, Jungle Jewel, Blackie and A Fist Is Not Everything have been published in Lost Tower anthologies in the UK during the past two years. Her themes of poetry range from nature, life, memories to thoughts, fantasy and love. Her poems are popular in the international poetry website.

关于作者

张次庚曾就读于北京首都师范大学英语专业，现以英文笔译为自由职业。

自2012年开始，她在国际诗歌网站上发表英文诗歌。她的诗歌《醉笑》《还剩下什么》《依然为你》《八点钟》《月亮诗人》自2013年以来在英国的“诗歌帮诗集”中相继出版。近两年，她的诗歌《狸猫》《丛林珠宝》《布莱奇》《拳头并非一切》在英国的“失去的塔”出版社出版。她的诗歌主题含括自然、生命、回忆、思绪、幻梦和爱，在国际诗歌网站受到欢迎。

About the Book

"Rouge in the Water" is my first collection of poetry. Most of the poems are my new works created in the past two years. I tried to expressed my true feelings and understanding on nature, life and love through my writing. I write in English in order to share my work with more international poetry lovers. So, this book is bilingual in English and Chinese. I hope the readers will more or less enjoy the beauty of it with emotional resonance.

关于诗集

《水中的胭脂》是我的第一本诗集，其中的作品大都是近两年的新作。

诗歌表达了我对自然、生命及爱的感悟。这几年我以英文写作，为的是能够使我的诗歌得到更多的国际诗歌爱好者的分享。因此，此书中我的诗歌为中英文对照。希望读者能在我的诗歌中或多或少地得到美的享受和情感共鸣。

Contents 目录

“Always write the first things uppermost in the heart”

—Allan Poe

“永远先写最初闪现在心头的东西”

—— 爱伦 · 坡

The Luminous Tadpoles

Night
is a dark river

Stars
are luminous tadpoles

Slowly moving
moving

Towards
the end of the dark

All is basked in the sun
after daybreak

发光的蝌蚪

夜
是一条黑暗的河

星星
是发光的蝌蚪

慢慢地移动
移动

朝着
黑暗的尽头

天亮后
一切都晒在阳光下

Lantern Festival

Red lanterns
Hung in mid–sky
The moon smiles

Milk Way opens
Many tiny nova stars
Drift out of the night

What a lively moment!
Amber eyes
Warm and sweet

Make a wish
At the festive night
Make a good wish

What's the best wish?
Come, come, quickly
Come the real spring

Let the vernal lights
Spread over the sky
Earth and heaven rejoice

灯节

红灯笼
挂在半空
月亮笑了

银河敞开
许多小新星
从夜幕中划出

多撩人啊！
琥珀色的眼睛
温暖又恬美

许一个愿吧
在节日的夜晚
许一个良愿吧

最好的愿望是什么
来吧，快来吧
真正的春天快来

让春光
洒满天空
大地和天穹齐欢

Rouge in the Water

In the lake water near a farmyard
Smiling faces mirrored in rouge red

Happy foreheads
Toward the upper reaches

A glimmer of warmth
Seeping into my breath

A stranger like me
Not feeling so lonely

Temporarily forget
I am alien here as a guest …

水中的胭脂

农庄附近的湖水中
映出许多张胭脂红的笑脸

幸福的额头
朝向上游

一丝暖意
渗入我的呼吸

像我这样的陌生人
并不感到那么孤寂

暂时忘了
我是异乡的异客

Something Delicate

you are delicate
as a porcelain pot

the entire body is fragile
please gently handle

when you are broken
you turn into a piece of ruin

your elegance just a pose
cannot withstand a single blow

精美

你精美得
像一把 细瓷茶壶

从上到下 脆弱
请轻拿轻放

一旦你被打碎
你就是一块块 废片

你的优雅只不过是一个姿势
不堪一击

Start and End

Start and end
Which is easier?
Day and night
Which is longer?

Say a word
As a start
Keep silent
As an end

The moon
Leaves a shadow
In front of
The morning sun

Start and end
Which is easier?
Day and night
Which is longer?

Which is easier?
Which is longer?
End and start
Day and night

开始和结束

开始和结束
哪一个更容易
白天和黑夜
哪一个更长

说出个只言片语吧
就算开始
保持沉默
就算结束

月亮
留下它的影子
在晨阳
前面

开始和结束
哪一个更容易
白天和黑夜
哪一个更长

哪一个更容易
哪一个更长
结束和开始
白天和黑夜

Still for You

The flower, scattered
The leaves, old
The riverbed, iced
You not yet appeared

The wind, heavy
The fog, hazy
The coral, reddened
I am coming in sincerity

Like a sheeny canary
I sing an easy ballad
Sing your name repeatedly
Along the road you passed

依然为你

花儿，碎了
叶儿，旧了
河床，冻了
你始终没有出现

风，沉了
雾，迷蒙了
珊瑚，变红了
我带着挚爱来了

就像一只闪亮的金丝雀
我唱着简单的歌谣
沿着你曾经走过的路
无数遍吟唱你的名字

The Earliest Flower's Talk

In March they knock at the door of Chun Ni
The Girl of Spring eagerly lets them in
One hundred flowers contend for beauty
Wait, wait, which one stands for her heart?
Listen! Listen to the subtle sound of flowering
Don't forget me – Don't forget me
I'll sweeten your vernal lips, my name is
Forget - Me - Not – Forget - Me - Not

最早的花语

三月 她们敲响了春妮的门
春姑娘迫不及待让她们进来
百花争艳
等等 等等 哪一朵称她的心呢?
听啊 听花开的柔曼声音
不要忘记我——不要忘记我
我要让你那春一般的唇更加甜美 我的名字是
勿忘我——勿忘我

Half World Away

Every day I see you
through a virtual window
Built in an air castle
Bridged by rainbow
When my sun rises
Moon is your pillow
A figure maps out a distance
Between us is oceanic farness
Half world away
I feel sad for reaching you no way
Cheer up! You once said –
Distance is nothing
as long as we build up a hope
within love, we are one

半个世界远

每天我透过一个虚拟的窗
看你
这扇窗架在空中阁楼
任彩虹连接
当我的太阳升起时
你却枕着月亮
地图上的一个数字标出了距离
我们之间 隔海之遥
半个世界远
我难过我们无法够到彼此
振作点儿！你曾经说——
距离算什么
只要我们心中存有希望和爱
就亲如一人

Mountain Lao

There is fairy fog
around the Mountain Lao

You look for an aged Taoist
I look for an old poet

In the thick mist
We want to have a result

That's why
We come

Oh, come over!
Look around!

The classical lyric
is in the creek

And the hermit
on the cloud

崂山

崂山
仙雾缭绕

你在寻找一位年迈的道士
我在寻找一位老诗人

在漫漫浓雾中
我们都想有一个结果

这正是我们来到此地的
缘由

哦！快来！
看哪！

古典的韵律
正流淌在小溪里

而隐士
坐在云端

Sarah

She smiled at me
Sunny
Dressed in red
Honey
Her eyelashes
Shiny
Ray of rainbow
Glary
Flying over
My joy
Make me
Naivety

莎拉

她对我笑
真灿烂
穿着红衣裳
好甜美
她的睫毛
闪着光
彩虹的光束
多荣耀
她正穿越着
我的喜悦
让我的心
变得天真

Little Owl

Do you like being lonely?
Why always be alone?
Tiny body stays at treetop
No dialogue to the moon
Keep watching with close attention
Midnight secret sharps your eyes
Your bright eyes see through
What happens on a dark screen
Hi little owl！
You are a silent creature
You boast to the deep night
No fear of waiting in the dark
Your wide and watchful eyes
Handsome as amber pearls

小猫头鹰

你喜欢孤独吗?
为什么总是独处?
小小的身体定在树梢上
盯着月亮一声不吭
保持高度的警觉
深夜的秘密擦亮你的眼睛
你那雪亮的眼睛看着
黑色银幕上发生的事
嗨 小猫头鹰!
你是一个沉默的小精灵
你向黑夜夸耀
你不怕黑暗中的守候
你聚精会神的眼眸
锃锃的 像琥珀色的珍珠

Como Island

Seabirds
Lining in a row
Parked at the wooden stakes

On the shallow shore
Moving steamers
No whistles to come

Dense trees
Surrounded by quietude
like a still fabric painting

Lake water
Close in sight
as if sky came

Clouds bird–viewed the sails
Sails chased the clouds
Clouds and sails leisured in sailing

Called on each other
An island
with no latch

科莫岛

水鸟
排成一排
停泊在木桩上

浅滩上
缓缓移动的汽船
隐匿了汽笛声

茂密的树林
静悄悄
如同一幅静止的布贴画

湖水
近在眼前
好似天空迎面扑来

云朵俯瞰白帆
白帆追逐着云朵
云和帆悠闲航行

云访帆 帆访云
一个没有门栓的
小岛

I Met Him at the No. 62 Square

I met him at the No. 62 Square
I said, "Hi, why aren't you in a museum?"
He said, "No, only wax people live in a museum
I am a tin soldier. My duty is on post always"

"Why on duty like this? You're famous in the world!
You should have been respected in a museum"

"No, my girl, I just want to stand here
I have been here for centuries
To help those who are in need
To safeguard those who are honest and kind-hearted
I am happy to be here like a firm Tin Soldier
Never to be down"

At the No. 62 Square I visited the brave Tin Soldier
I remembered him as a true soldier rather than a legend

我在第 62 广场遇见了他

我在第 62 广场遇见了他
我说，嗨，为什么你不在一个博物馆里？
他说，不，只有蜡像才会住在博物馆
我是一个小锡兵，我的职责是永远站岗

为什么要站岗？你可是大有名气的啊！
你本应该在一个博物馆里受到世人瞻慕

不，我只想站在这里
我已守在这里一个世纪了
甘愿帮助那些需要帮助的人
保护那些善良和诚实的人
我很高兴我在这里就像一个坚定的小锡兵
从不失望

在第 62 广场我拜访了勇敢的小锡兵
我将永远记得他是一个真正的士兵而不只是一个传说

Unsealed Letter

Dear Water Cuff
I sat by the fish tank
Dazing at the colorful fish
How the water creatures
Row their cruise
Do you drink coconut juice?
Do you eat ice cream?
I have the things you may love
Hope you appear soon
Bring me some funny jokes
My river is frozen outside
Cannot read
Any living story
A winter–sleep riverbank
No surprise to jump out
Dear Water Cuff
Would you help me out ?
through this winter
through my fantasy

没有封口的信

亲爱的水卡夫先生
我坐在鱼缸旁
呆呆地望着彩色的鱼
看它们如何划过自己的巡游
你喝椰汁吗?
吃冰激凌吗?
我有好多你喜欢的东西
真想你能立即出现
带给我几段笑话
外面的河水已封冻
读不到任何生动的轶事
冬眠的河床
没有惊喜跳出
亲爱的水卡夫先生
你能不能帮帮我
挨过这个冬天
挨过我的空想

Follow Each Other

Clouds followed me onward
They needed a shepherd
I tried to climb to the hilltop
They followed me climbing the top

I was tired
Slowly down
Then I followed
Behind the clouds

I needed a sunbonnet
They read my mind
opened their dust coat
Covering on my head

Clouds followed me onward
Well, I too followed
We walked through a long day
through a season, through this way

相随

云跟着我往上爬
它们需要一个牧羊人
我试图爬到山顶
它们跟着我向山顶爬

我累了
慢下来
跟在云后

我需要一把阳伞
云读懂了我的心思
它们敞开自己的风衣
遮挡在我的头上

云跟着我向上攀
时而，我也跟着云
我们走过了一天
走过了一季，以这样的方式走过

A Pasted Picture

You pasted our pictures into one
As if we had stayed in the same scene
Clouds drifted over the polar flowers
Cheerful smiles twinkled at moonrise
Heart was rippling like tides
Eyes did never tell lies
Come to me! You said to the picture
Come to my dream! My darling there ...

一张粘贴的照片

你把我们的照片粘在一起
好像我们身处同一个场景
云朵飘过极地花
欢快的笑容在月光下闪烁
心如潮水在荡漾
眼睛从来不说谎
到我这里来吧！你对着相片说
到我的梦里来吧！我的挚爱……

When Our Coach Rode through the Wildernes

When our coach drove along the wide wild fields
My eyes were captured by the endless greenness
Delicate fragrance overflew through the land of grass
Such a scented air and scenery I longed to last long
The emerald green reminded me of the youth be bygone
The prime time in a life journey seemed passing very soon
It was like an instant in an autumn, a fitful wind swept
Blowing away the brilliant green but a barren desert was left

当我们的大巴车穿过原野

我们的大巴车沿着辽阔的原野行驶
我的视线被一望无际的绿野捕获
风中飘来清纯的草香味
我渴望这样香醇的空气和景色久留
绿色让我想起过往的青春
最好的生命阶段在人生旅途中那么匆匆
就像秋天的一瞬，一阵秋风掠过
迅速带走了这片绿野，留下荒芜

Resounding Wings

my heart
wants to fly
to a penthouse
built in the clouds

what lies
around the penthouse
the hopeful air
for rootless flowers

my dream
never ceases
roaming
into such a place

I want to be
my own chanting bird
dare to wish
for a pair of resounding wings

响亮的翅膀

我的心
想要飞
飞到一个镶嵌在云端的
楼阁

楼阁周围
有着什么
哈 充满希望的空气
滋养无根的花

我的梦
从未停止
漫游到
这样一方净土

我想成为
我自己的歌姬鸟
敢于期待一双
响亮的翅膀

The Night after Snowfall

—inspired by Daniel's "Snowfall for Cigeng"

Whose heart is singing for the lily snowflakes?
A lemon colored lamp is mirrored on the undefiled ice
Frozen eyelashes turn to crystal–clear butterflies
Twinkling in the snow - flashing in the darkness

雪后的夜晚

——有感于美国诗人丹尼尔的诗“飘雪 给次庚”

谁的心在为这洁白的雪花歌唱?
一盏柠檬色的灯映在无瑕的冰上
沾着冰凌的睫毛变成晶莹的蝴蝶
在雪中一闪一闪——在黑夜中闪

Flying over the Rape Flowers

This is a shimmering western plain in late May
A large tract of rape flowers yellowing as gold
The woman in white gown walked by softly
A chic bird from afar soared to the sky like a meteor

飞越油菜花

这是一个五月末的闪亮的西方平原
大片大片的油菜花黄灿灿宛若金子
一个穿着白色长裙的女人轻轻走过
一只来自远方的鸟像流星一样飞过

Isn't It the Last Summer?

The wheels on his wheelchair
Rolling over the moving sun
A ceramic plate, blue and old
Covered with shattered lilacs
Today is Saturday, someone
Wears a pair of fisherman's shoes
The weather no good, too cold
A hasty rain beats on his breath
Wind plays with running shadows
He wonders if he rides on a cloud
The petals quietly lie in the plate
The dying aroma is much to be pitied

难道这是最后一个夏天吗？

他轮椅上的轮子
在移动的太阳上滚动
一个瓷盘，钴蓝而老旧
盛满破碎的紫丁香
今天是星期六，有人
穿着一双渔夫鞋
天气不好，太冷了
匆忙的雨敲打着他的呼吸
风吹着奔跑的影子
他想知道他是否骑在云上
花瓣静静地躺在盘子里
垂死的香气楚楚怜人

Christmas Glow

I learned my first Christmas carol from you
The Twelve Days of Christmas
And then the other affecting song –
I Am Dreaming of a White Christmas
Your name is not forgotten
A nice name – the Snowy Sunlight was you

Beautiful hymns
Beautiful Christmas
Beautiful memories
Beautiful snowy sunlight
Where are you the long gone snowy sunlight?
May I sing these songs to you?

My voice is not changed
My accent is not changed
You taught me all of these
I would say that every year
I say Merry Christmas on the day
Now I say to you –

圣诞之光

我学会的第一首圣诞颂歌是你教给我的
“圣诞季的十二天”
还有另外一首动人的歌——
“我梦想有一个白色的圣诞节”
我没有忘记你的名字
一个好听的名字——你是白霞

美丽的赞美诗
美丽的圣诞节
美丽的记忆
美丽的圣洁之光
你在哪里啊久违的白霞?
我可以为你唱这些圣歌吗?

我的声音没有变
我的口音没有变
你教会我这一切
我每一年在这一天都会说
圣诞快乐
现在我对你说——

Merry Christmas
Merry Snowy Sunlight
I Am Dreaming of a White Christmas
I am missing you the joyful glow
Merry Christmas
My True Love Sent to You

圣诞快乐

白霞快乐

我梦想有一个白色的圣诞节

我想念你这欢乐之光

圣诞快乐

我真诚的爱全都给你

Years Are Fine

thinking about the future
I am going to cry
but I won't let you
capture my tears

we only have today
or yesterday
no future – you say
once in your drama line

岁月静好

想到以后
我想流泪
但我不会让你
捕捉到我的眼泪

我们只有今天
或昨天
没有未来——你说
在你的一句台词里你如是说

On the Last Day

You said, you would soon get rid of light
In the dark, you would feel more peaceful

That day, you said so in a weak voice
But I did not understand you fully

So, I said easily, is it? Oh I liked light
Especially the twinkling light in your eyes

You said nothing more, then
Closed your eyes quietly

From that moment
Your world was no light but only angles

I felt very sorry I failed to make out your last word
Unaware of the power of a heart on the verge of a lightless wor

最后一天

你说，你很快就会摆脱光
在黑暗中，你会感到更安宁

那天，你用一种微弱的声音这样说
可是我并没有完全领会你的意思

所以，我不经意地说，是吗？哦，我喜欢光
尤其喜欢你眼中闪烁的光

你没有再说什么，然后
静静地闭上了眼睛

从那一刻起
你的世界不再有光，只有天使

我感到非常难过我没有意会你最后的话
没有意识到一颗濒临无光世界边缘的勇敢之心

Empty Valley

Red reed, White River Valley
A stunning gouache in my eyes
I leaned on the window of the valley
Let the breeze sweep across my face
I stood on the huge canvas
Slowly closing my eyes —
Pretending it was your gentle fingers
Caressing on my cheeks
I loved this unexpected tenderness
So I came to believe blindly
I had met you in the empty valley
When I thought of you, I was not lonely

空谷

红色的芦苇，白河谷
我眼中的一幅水粉画
我倚在山谷的窗口
任萧萧的风拂过我的脸
我站在巨大的画布上
慢慢地闭上我的眼睛
假装是你温柔的手指
轻抚着我的脸颊
我爱这意想不到的温柔
所以我竟然相信
我曾在这山谷里遇到你
当我想你的时候，我不孤独

Yunnan Tie–Dyed Cloth

Chaotic background
Vivacious colours
Lips plump and rosy
Eye–catching red like canna petals
Exposing from a long air ladder
She, not speaking a single word
Her lips moist as morning dews
Water lily opened on her hair
She shyly plucked the water lily
Put the flower between her lips

云南扎染

眼花缭乱的背景
绚丽多彩
丰满而瑰丽的唇
扎眼得像红色的大丽花瓣
自一个柔曼的天梯上
娇容显露
她 沉默不语
双唇滋润宛若晨露
水莲花开在她的发髻上
她害羞地摘下水莲花
将花朵衔在唇间

Will you love a poet?

Sometimes the rhythm of the poem is cheerful
Like a singing brook in the valley very delightful

Sometimes the melody of the poem is melancholy
Like a distant moon behind a hillside very lonely

O, poetry – brook – and moon –
Lyrical, gurgling, and brooding

Poetry is from the heart of a poet
Will you ever listen to the giggling brook?

Will you ever see through the silent moon?
Will you go close to a poet – touch his heart?

你会爱上一位诗人吗

有时候 诗歌的节奏是欢快的
宛如一条欢唱的小溪在山谷中徜徉

有时候 诗歌的旋律是忧伤的
好像山峦背后遥远的月亮那般孤寂

呵 诗歌啊——小溪——月亮——
时而抒情 时而缠绵 时而感伤

诗歌是诗人的心啊
你曾听到过汀汀流音吧？

你曾凝视过沉静的月亮吧
你会不会走近诗人的心——感触这颗心?

SNOWFALL for Cigeng (By Daniel, the USA©)

Today the snow fell for hours
across southern Minnesota. And it did not
hesitate for even a moment until everything was
covered in thick, pure white flakes. Oh, how close
Heaven seemed as that snow closed the gap
between earth and sky! Through it I walked
three–legged like the third figure in the riddle
the Sphinx posed to bold Oedipus, my cane
steadying my steps as it discovered buried links
of a vanished pathway. I must trust so many things:
the ground's firm base, the mild air, the intelligence
of a mere mortal, the sky looming over me, with an alien
beauty I try to comprehend. And I know, you too see
the alien sky of winter, and it comforts me beyond language
to know this. There is no fear inside me nor is there any
inside you, not even if a new Sphinx posed a new riddle.

飘雪 给次庚（©丹尼尔，美国）

今天雪下了好几个钟头
横飘明尼苏达南部 没有
片刻的犹豫，飘啊飘直到一切都
覆盖在厚厚的纯白色的雪片下。哦，多么贴近
白雪近乎关闭了天堂与大地的距离
地球和天空之间竟没有缝隙！漫步在雪中
三条腿像谜语中的第三个数字
大胆的俄狄浦斯构成的狮身人面像，我的拐杖
让我的步伐稳健 让我的脚发现了在消失的小径上
隐匿的踪迹 我必须相信许多事情：
坚实的大地 柔和的空气 一个凡人的
智慧 天空笼罩着我，我试图理解一种
陌生的美 我知道，你也看到
冬天异样的天空，它给我的安慰无法用言语表达
在我心里没有恐惧，在你心里也没有惧怕
就连新的狮身人面像提出的新的谜题也不惧怕

(Tr. Cigeng —— 次庚翻译）

Temple Fair

I was in the streams of people
Busily coming and going
I wanted to find a Totem mask
Might be hung on an eave of tiles
Afternoon sunshine was like a sword
Dazzling, sharp, piercing to my eyes
Yet, chill stirred the early spring air
Crazy wind of the northland blew hard
Colorful flags of silk carps flew on high
My hair fluttered as a carp–flag of black
I followed the crowd to look for the mask
If seeing the mask, I must have believed
That would be a good omen, a good sign
Long long ago, a royal girl of 17 years old
Wearing the odd mask on her innocent face
Strolling around the fair, the same afternoon
She happened to meet her future lover
People said that was an auspicious symbol
Good luck to me! Could I find the mask soon?
To have the rare face on my face – give me luck

庙会

我在熙熙攘攘的人群中
穿梭
我要找到一个图腾面具
它或许就挂在瓦檐上
午后的阳光像一把利剑
炫灿 锋锐 刺入我的眼
然而，春寒料峭
北国的风狂劲地吹
彩色的鲤鱼旗高高飞扬
我的头发便是黑色的鲤鱼旗
我夹杂在人群中寻找那个面具
如果看到面具，我一定相信
这将是一个好兆头 一个好迹象
很久以前 一位十七岁的皇家女孩
在她天真的脸上戴上了古怪的面具
她就是这样在集市上走着，同一个下午
她邂逅了她的心上人
人们说那是一个吉祥的象征
祝我好运吧！我能很快找到面具吗？
稀罕的面具戴在我脸上——带给我好运

My Old Piggy Bank

A little boy was watering some purple flowers
on a handmade small round shaped coin box
Father said, his age is the same as yours
How wonderful! I'm eight years old, he's eight, too
I said to my father in my naive voice

This was the first gift my father sent to me
A boy, at my age according to my father
Watering purple flowers for my piggy bank, ah
He does his job, so you do your job, father said

But I never put a penny in my piggy bank
Fortunately, father never checked the box
I often watched the boy watering his purple flowers
and wiped the piggy bank with my clothes

我的老存钱罐

一个小男孩在给一些紫色的花浇水
在一个手工制作的小圆形存钱罐上
父亲说，小男孩的年纪和你一样大
太好了！我八岁，他也八岁呀
我用稚幼的声音对父亲说

这是父亲送给我的第一个礼物
一个小男孩，按我父亲说的，和我同岁
在我的存钱罐上浇着紫色的花，啊哈
他做他的事，所以你要做你的事，父亲说

可是我从未往存钱罐里放进过一分钱
幸好父亲没有检查我的这个钱罐子
我常常看着小男孩浇灌他的紫色花
然后用我的衣服将存钱罐擦得锃新

Port

the Port
is gray
the tears of farewell
dye it gray

the ship
tears off the waves
coastline
is trembling

when to come back?
your wandering heart
the port
will wait for long

港口

港口
总是灰蒙蒙的
告别的眼泪
把它染成灰色

船儿
撕开了海水
海岸线
在颤抖

何时回来
你的漂泊的心
港口
将永远等候

Regret

Don't ask for forgiveness, he's gone
Happiness is no longer with a rosy shine
What stirring in memories is the pain
We are already the fallen leaves
away from the tree, once in luxuriantly green
But now with a twinge of resentment

遗憾

不要祈求原谅，他已离开
快乐不再是玫瑰色
痛苦搅拌在回忆里
我们都已是坠落的树叶
离开了曾经郁郁葱葱的树
而现在却有一点点怨恨

In Memory of June

that day
I was so sad
all the stars in the sky
blurred like my teary eyes

that day
something was unusual
dahlias put out the dawning ray
scarlet red burned your blood vessel

that day
was a sticky June's day
I failed to catch your final voice
attached to the vocal cord of angel's

六月的怀念

那一天
我如此悲伤
天上的星星都变得模糊
就像我泪蒙蒙的眼

那一天
有些不寻常
大丽花熄灭了黎明的光
猩红燃烧你的血管

那一天
是一个粘热的六月天
我没能听见你最后的声音
它附在了天使的声带上

Rootless Flower

You are a rootless flower
When wind becomes calmer
You bloom into fullness

You are straying petals
When wind turns into a roar
You open bigger and bigger

You have no fragrance
But make my eyes illusory
I want to feed you with my tears

无根的花

你是一朵无根的花
当风儿变得平静
你就完全绽放

你是飘离的花瓣
当风怒吼
你就越开越大

你虽没有花香
却迷幻了我的眼睛
我想用我的泪水滋养你

Energy

When I could hardly hold on
You appear in my mind
You always cheer me up
That was a frightening channel
Swimming cross you struggled
Lonely, unexpected
First time, exhausted
An inconceivably long journey
in the bone bone–chilling cold water

You were more difficult than me
You were doing like a mighty warrior

When I am in despair
You give me enlightenment
I remember the lines you read to me—
Despair is a kind of power to an extent
while the hope, is of incompetent

When I could almost give up my heart
You appear in my mind
Because of you I find my source of energy!

能量

每当我撑不住的时候
你就出现在我的脑海
你总是令我打起精神
那是一个难以征服的海峡
你奋力游过去
孤独 难以预料
第一次，筋疲力尽
不可思议的漫长征程
在冰冷刺骨的海水里

你比我更难
可你做得像一个强悍的勇士

我在绝望的时候
你给我启示
我记得你读过的一句话——
绝望有绝望的力量
就如同希望有希望的无能

当我就要放弃的时候
你就浮现在我的心里
因为你，我有了一种力量的源泉！

Pen Pal on the Cloud

Cloud
like a piece of cream
pasted
in my early morning sky

I opened my window
surprisingly seeing
your handwriting
imprinted on the cream

Cherish Every Single Day –
Hey, I Wish You a Good Day!

I read your words
eagerly collecting
your strokes
and forgot the creamy cloud

Then I held a red candle
for you, silently praying
I came to believe
You had read my blazing heart

云上的笔友

云
像一块奶油
粘在
我清晨的天空

我打开窗
惊讶地看到
你的笔迹
烙在奶油上

珍惜每一天！
嗨，祝你好心情！

我读了你的话
急切地收集
你的笔触
把奶油云忘在了脑后

然后，我捧着一支红蜡烛
为你，默默祈祷
我愿意相信
你读到了我这颗炽热的心

One–Line Tide

"tang ba la lai yi ka"
The sea came to the shore

"tang ba la lai yi ka"
The sea receded from the shore

She sang the song
among her two hundred songs

One–line lyric only
Simply

She was twelve years old
Running along the seaside

Repeated rhythm of the tide
Patting her feet naughtily

"tang ba la lai yi ka"
"tang ba la lai yi ka …"

The sea rushed to the shore
The sea withdrew from the shore

一行潮汐

“唐巴拉莱依卡”
海水聚到了岸边

“唐巴拉莱依卡”
海水从岸边退去

她唱这首歌
她的二百首歌曲中的一首

只有一行歌词
如此简单

她十二岁
沿着海边跑

潮汐的重复韵律
顽皮地拍打着她的脚

“唐巴拉莱依卡”
“唐巴拉莱依卡”

大海冲到岸边
大海又从它的咆哮中撤退了

Cobblestone

The cobbles are tiny stars in the river
Their delicate light spread on the ripple

A kid holding a small bamboo basket
Come to pick up the cobbles in sunset

Out of the water, bring them to his place
"Hey, the cobbles are just some oval stones"

鹅卵石

鹅卵石是河水中的星星
细润的光泽点缀在波漪上

一个小童提着小竹篮
在夕阳下拾着鹅卵石

小童从水中捞出鹅卵石，带回家
嗨，这不过是一堆椭圆形的石头啊

Cover Page

I began to think of a vague scene
He let me in after I'd soundly slept
Spider–plant grew with new leaves
Climbing the rim of my glaze vase
Faint scent diffusing in the house
It came from a biting cold season
Soaked in water the roots intricate
I began to think of a vague face
Bud of February, in quietness
Dogwood of June, in gloominess
His lips always closed tight
I did not hear any voice, yet
I saw he used a bunch of violet
Drawing a light purple morning
A pure purple morning, ah morning
The morning illuminated my vision

封面

我开始想起一个模糊的场景
他让我熟睡之后进来了
吊兰长出了新嫩的叶子
爬上了我的釉花瓶的边
房子里弥漫着淡淡的香味
香气来自一个寒冷的季节
浸泡在水中的根 错综繁复
我开始想起一张模糊的脸
二月的蓓蕾是静雅的
六月的山茱萸是忧伤的
他的嘴唇总是紧闭着
我没有听到任何声音 却
看见他用一束紫罗兰
画出一个淡紫色的早晨
一个清纯的紫色的早晨，晨啊
这个早晨照亮了我的视线

Courage

I bought a poetry book on a winter day
On the cover page I noted down the date
When the trees regenerated, I thought
I'd tell you about the courage of the poet

She said she always admired the courage of an insect
So I added my words on the page of inside --

My hands are empty and dry in winter
Like the bald trees listless and bare
But the little insect has carried his food home
Sleeping soundly in a restful secret lair...

勇气

一个冬日 我买了一本诗集
在封页上 我写下了日期
当树木重生，我想
我会告诉你诗人的勇气

她说她总是羡慕一种昆虫的勇气
所以我在内页上加上了我的话——

冬天 我两手空空 干枯枯
像光秃秃的枝桠无精打采
而小昆虫却把自己的食粮带回了家
安睡在宁静的秘密巢穴中 ……

Ant

Ants carry their stolen food quietly
towards a delicious time, no one knows
home is hidden in a burrow

蚂蚁

蚂蚁悄悄地搬运着偷来的食物
朝着一个美味的时刻行进
没人知道家藏在一个地洞里

Candlelight

candlelight went out
scent lingering in midnight
lovesick heart burning

烛光

烛光熄灭
烛香萦绕午夜
思念的心燃烧

Ao Sen Park (1)

Alvin said
There were many birds
in Ao Sen Park

Leila and I, excited
Then, to the park
to see birds

Alvin said
He had seen
over ten sorts of birds

Oh poor us
Only saw three kinds
Sparrow, cuckoo, magpie

Alvin said
He came in October
We, in December

奥森公园（1）

阿尔汶说
奥森公园里
有许多鸟

蕾拉和我有点兴奋
然后 就去了奥森
去看鸟

阿尔汶说
那天他看到了
十几种鸟

呵 可怜的我们
只看到三种
麻雀 布谷 喜鹊

阿尔汶说
他是十月来的
而我们 是十二月

Birds had good memory
Felt a bit contented
At least we saw a magpie

We told Alvin
We met some magpies!
Our lifelong happy bird …

鸟儿有良好的记忆
我们感到了一点点满足
至少我们看到了喜鹊

我们告诉阿尔汶
遇到了喜鹊!
我们永远的幸运鸟

Ao Sen Park (2)

The lake was gurgling
like a jade–like sleeve
Winding at the foot of mountain

The willow turned mature
like the braid of autumn
Swaying in the soothing air

The sun looked contented
Combing the golden long hair
Ao Sen Park gave me warmth in September

Birds were flying above my head
I once said
"Birds have good memory"

They landed on the green grass
Near me, once, twice, triple times
I listened to the birds' twitters

I always waited for the birds to come
I would tell Alvin my dear friend
I saw ten birds, at least ten, more than last time

奥森公园（2）

湖水淙淙
像一条玉袖
缠绕在山脚下

柳树茵茵
像秋天的发辫
在舒缓的空气中轻荡

太阳看上去称心如意
梳理着自己的金色长发
九月的奥森公园带给了我暖意

鸟儿 在我头顶上飞过
我曾经说过
鸟儿的记性可好了

它们降落在悠悠青草上
接近我，一次，两次，三次
我听着鸟儿的鸣唱

我总是等待鸟儿来到
我会告诉阿尔汶 我亲爱的朋友
我看见了十只鸟，比上次多

Ao Sen Park (3)

Magpies fly around the heaven for another 365 laps
The arms of the torch tower touch the clouds
Do not blame me I am escaping from my poetry
Once again to watch your real cartoon shown in your entry

A northern mallard paddles in the rippling lake
Her lover chases her hard with his feathers' shake
The silk–like water is a huge silvery blue screen
The wave of water is the lovers' rhythm of dancing

The poplars I saw last year are still tall and straight
Beside them little newborn relatives around in sight
Buds of peach blossoms tiny like red beans
Who is thinking of the most beloved on earth?

How many green memories the trees cast in the three years
How many unsure skies the birds fly over in their flying time
At the beginning of the sunset evening prayer starts
The heartfelt whisper is heard in the new vernal breeze …

奥森公园（3）

喜鹊绕着天堂又飞了三百六十五圈
火炬塔的手臂触到了云端
不要怪我 我逃离了我的诗章
再一次来看你的真实的动画

北方的绿头鸭在拍打着湖水
爱侣追逐在她身后 奋力抖动着翅膀
丝绸般的湖水是巨大的宝蓝色银幕
涟漪起伏是恋人们的舞蹈节奏

去年我看到的杨树依然挺立
身旁围绕着新生的小亲戚
桃花骨朵幼小如红豆
谁在思念尘世中的一个挚爱?

一棵树在三年的光阴里洒下多少绿色的回忆?
一只鸟在三年里飞过了多少无常的天空?
晚祷在晚霞中开始
心中的呢喃在新春的微风中传送

Alive

Autumn gone
Take away the leaves

Leaves gone
Take away a golden season

Golden season gone
Take away the warmth

Warmth gone
Take away a heart

Heart gone
Take away the love

Love gone
Take away a promise

Promise gone
Take away the voice

Voice gone
Take away the echo

活着

秋天走了
带走了叶子

叶子走了
带走了金色季节

金色季节走了
带走了暖意

暖意走了
带走了一颗心

心走了
带走了爱

爱走了
带走了诺言

诺言走了
带走了声音

声音走了
带走了回音

Echo gone
Take away the memories

Memories gone
Take away the colors

Colors gone
Take away the scenery

Scenery gone
Take away the birds

Birds gone
Take away the wings

Wings gone
Take away the freedom

Freedom gone
Take away the soul

Soul gone
Take away the body

Body gone

回音走了
带走了回忆

回忆走了
带走了色彩

色彩走了
带走了景致

景致走了
带走了鸟儿

鸟儿走了
带走了翅膀

翅膀走了
带走了自由

自由走了
带走了灵魂

灵魂走了
带走了肉体

肉体走了

Take away the balance

Balance gone
Take away the direction

Direction gone
Take away the pursuit

Pursuit gone
Take away the dream

Dream gone
Take away the hope

Hope gone
Take away the spirit

Spirit gone
Take away the life

Oh, No, No, No!
But, Please!

Don't take all away
I am still alive

We are still alive
Leave to us a bit, to hold

带走了平衡

平衡走了
带走了方向

方向走了
带走了追求

追求走了
带走了梦想

梦想走了
带走了希望

希望走了
带走了精神

精神走了
带走了生命

哦，不不不！
请不要这样

不要将一切都带走
我还活着

我们还活着
请留下一点点

A Wild Dog in Chong'li

When I caught a sight of him
He was climbing up a coal hill
I was curious why he stayed in the coal hill
I watched him while he soon reached the top
The dazzling sunlight was very sharp
That made me difficult to open my eyes
But I did not give up staring at him
He now was lying on the top of the coal
Lazily like a small baby, he licked his paws
The midday sun like quilt pretty warm
Under the sun he found him a home
No matter good or bad, the sun is his all

崇礼的狗

当我瞥见它的那一刹那
它正向一座煤山顶爬去
我好奇它为什么要待在黑煤山上
于是我盯着它 而它很快就到达了顶端
阳光炫亮
刺得我几乎睁不开眼
但我的目光一直没有离开它
它可好，正慵懒地躺在煤山顶
像个婴宝宝，舔着自己的小爪
正午的太阳就像暖和和的被子
狗儿在阳光下找到了一个家
无论好坏，阳光就是一切

A Village at J'Ming Station

By the hillside the car stopped
The remote village was in sight
Bowing to your aged forehead
I bended over to look at an old gate

It was already an empty place
No kinsman lived here for years
Shabby adobe houses, ruined
Northern trees stood in the yard

Dark green leaves shone in sunset
Nothing dazzling could compete
What you've reserved is the last gold
Under your feet, the root, pretty solid

鸡鸣驿的村庄

车子停在了小山坡上
我终于见到了久远的村庄
我向它的苍老额头致敬
弯下身看着一个老门墩儿

已是一个空荡荡的地方
多年了 已不再有亲朋住在这里
破旧的房屋 残毁了
北方的树孤立在院子里

幽绿的树叶在夕阳里闪烁
没有什么比这更耀眼炫目
你所保留的是这最后的金黄
在你的脚下 根 坚固如初

My Drifting Bottle

The brook murmurs
Carrying away
Your own song

I put a drifting bottle
In the brook, inside fills
My long poem

Water takes it away till far
Drifting bottle is broken
Poem sinks to the bottom

No one knows who I am
No one cares I have a poem
But I know where I am with you

漂泊瓶

小溪潺潺
带走了
你的歌

我放了一只漂泊瓶
在水里 瓶中装有
我的长诗

溪水带它到很远的地方
漂泊瓶碎了
诗沉到水底

没人知道我是谁
没人在意我有一首诗
而我却知道我在哪里和你在一起

I Light Twelve Red Candles for You Now

I hold twelve red candles in my hands
Hope you would see me from the skies
Twelve forms a circle – a round is perfect
You are not in the place I used to know
I am still in the old lane you once knew
Look for me, please! I am a bright red halo
around your penthouse through moonlight
Come to find me! Come to see my tender blaze!
I am shimmering to give you my warmest heart
Long live, my love, my fondest love will last

我为你点亮了十二支红蜡烛

我捧着十二支红蜡烛
想着你会在云端看到我
十二是一个轮回 圆是完美的
你已不在我曾经知晓的地方
而我还在你熟悉的老巷子
你找我吧 我现在是一个红色的光晕
围绕着你那月光笼罩的空中楼阁
来找我吧 来看我的温柔火焰
我闪着的光给你我最温暖的心
万岁，我的爱，我最深情的爱延绵长久

Farmer and Poet

They plant vegetables
They do not plant spring
They plant the soil of life

They plant spring
They do not plant vegetables
They plant the dream of heart

They plant what they love
Vegetables, spring, and life
Live on their creation, alive

农夫和诗人

他们种植蔬菜
他们没有种植春天
他们却种了一种生命的土壤

他们种植春天
他们没有种植蔬菜
他们却种了一颗梦之心

他们种植他们所爱的东西
蔬菜 春天 和生命
他们仰仗自己的造物，活着

Hardy Canna by the River

The shore grows with hardy cannas, river thawed
I believe everything is going to be tender …
Is there someone coming to hold my hand?
The shore grows with hardy cannas, river thawed
Who can capture the vernal queen as a winner ?
A splendid time is elapsing along with quicksand

The shore grows with hardy cannas, river thawed
I believe everything is going to be tender …

岸边的美人蕉

岸边长出美人蕉，河流解冻
我相信一切都会变得温柔……
会有人来牵我的手吗?
岸边长出美人蕉，河流解冻
谁能捕获春之女皇而成为一个胜利者
一个辉煌的时刻正在随着流沙流逝

岸边长出美人蕉，河流解冻
我相信一切都会变得温柔……

Haiku（1）

far higanbana
spreads into farther distance
sky grows a pink shore

俳句（1）

遥远的彼岸花
延伸到更远的地方
天空诞出一片粉红色的海岸

Haiku (2)

this winter no gift
snow is frozen in fable
poet fainted in poems

俳句（2）

这个冬天没有礼物
雪被寓言封住
诗人在诗中昏了过去

Mama

I am in the June valley
Waiting for a call of destiny
Floating by, floating by
A dawn of peony so shiny
No doubt there is a paradise
A belle like a fairy, how funny!
She has a name – Coral Belle
I am in the June valley
Touching her hands tied on clouds

妈妈

我在六月谷
等待命运的召唤
飘啊飘 飘过来的是
牡丹色的曙光，如此闪亮
毫无疑问，有一个天堂
有一位宛若仙女的美人，多有趣！
她有一个名字——珊瑚美人
我在六月谷
试图拉住她绑在云上的手

Unique

You are different from the others
Why, you look so deep and heavy
Your artery turns into inky color
The hills around you are all lively
Green, young, at odds with you
You stand like a giant inkstone
When the dark falls, they get dim
You do fear nothing, your luster
Become the eyes of the hills, shine

独特

你与众不同
为什么你看起来如此深沉和凝重
你的脉搏变成漆黑的颜色
你周围的群山都显得活络
青翠 年轻 与你格格不入
你屹立着像一个巨大的砚石
当黑暗降临，他们变得暗淡
而你什么都不怕，你的光泽
成了山的眼睛，璀璨夺目

Looking for a Cicada

midsummer comes
cicada sings
I start to look for cicada
on the gorgeous trees

he chirps his bright song
to wake up a dreary summer
I always love to hear the chirping
but could hardly find him

I stand under the branches
to look for the cicada
along the track of the summer voice
coming from the towering poplars

寻找蝉

仲夏来临
知了鸣唱
我开始在华丽的树上
寻找蝉

他唱着清亮的歌
催醒了沉闷的夏
我总是爱听蝉鸣叫
却找不到他的踪影

我站在树下
沿着来自冲天杨的
仲夏之声频道
寻找蝉

The Moon, the Poet

What is behind the poet?
A lonely heart through a night

What is behind the moon?
A crystal teardrop on a stone

The poet takes out his heart
He retains nothing

The tears shed from the stone
She says nothing

The poet stares at the moon
Heart in pain

The moon looks at the poet
Tears sweeten

月亮，诗人

诗人背后是什么？
是一颗穿过黑夜的心

月亮背后是什么？
是石头上落下的一颗晶莹的泪滴

诗人掏出他的心
他什么也没有留下

眼泪从石头上淌下
她什么也没有说

诗人凝望月亮
心好痛

月亮看着诗人
眼泪变甜了

Memory of Love

No eaves
No frames
Your terrace full of starlight

No oath
No artful mouth
I read your soul–searching eyes

Memory is the movie–like slow motion
Replayed in a crumpled screen
I am the flying moth that darts into the scene

爱的记忆

没有檐
没有框
你的露台满是星光

没有誓言
没有巧嘴
我读到你穿透灵魂的眼睛

回忆就像电影的慢动作
在起皱的银幕上回放
我是一只飞蛾扑进场景

Coral Cloud

No matter how deep the sky is to hide
I will always stand under the sky
Waiting for an endless stream of coral cloud
to emerge, adrift into my longing eyes
It is a secret between you and me, hey
You would never laugh at me in such a daze

珊瑚云

无论天空藏匿多深
我都会站在苍穹下
等待层出不穷的珊瑚云
出现，飘进我渴望的眼睛
这是我俩之间的秘密，嘿
你也就不会笑我傻傻发呆了

If We Have

if having joy, share it
if having wine, taste it

if having seed, sowing it
if having spring, embrace it

if having dream, ride on it
if having courage, hold it

if having love, say it out
if having hatred, erase it

if having moonlight, sip it
if having poetry, chant it

time waits for no man
time is flying

如果我们有

如果有快乐，分享它
如果有佳酿，品尝它

如果有种子，播下它
如果有春天，拥抱它

如果有梦想，乘着它
如果有勇气，抓住它

如果有爱，就说出来
如果有恨，抹去它

如果有月光，就喝一口吧
如果有诗，就唱吧

时不我待
时间飞逝

Shanghai Breeze

A girl sings her song of September
with a French phoenix tree together

I'm just watching the falling leaves
Autumn wind blows away the butterflies

They are the old faces of the tree
The girl's hands hold the lonely tree

I pick up the fallen leaves
She smiles at me in distance

I begin to sow the fallen leaves
Softly on her new footsteps

上海微风

一个女孩唱着九月的歌
她在和法国梧桐一起唱

我恰好在观赏纷飞的落叶
秋风却吹走了蝴蝶

它们都是树上老去的脸啊
女孩的手抱着孤独的树

我捡起落叶
她在远处对我笑

我开始播撒落叶
轻轻地，在她新的脚步上

Father

So far, I've seen you cry
Only once in my life

It was on her funeral day
You sat in a wheelchair

Your hand caressed her face
I supported your body

Your tears rolling down the face
Dropped on the back of my hands

I never felt such cold tears
Like icy water

I held back my tears
Looking at your face

Your face, like a statue
A statue crying into pieces

父亲

此生的我
只见你哭过一次

是葬礼那天
你坐在轮椅上

你的手抚摸着她的脸
我撑着你的身体

你的眼泪滚过你的脸颊
滴在我的手背上

我从未感受过如此冰冷的眼泪
冷若冰水

我忍住我的泪水
望着你的脸

你的脸像一座雕像
一座哭碎的雕像

To Adapt

We have the wounds
So, love the sunray to caress
We run into the haze
So, love the heavy wind to blow
We love you
So we long for you
Oh you come, you've come
Not because you love us
Just because, you pass
through, only by chance?

适应

我们有伤
所以，爱阳光的抚慰
我们闯入雾霾
所以，爱强劲的风吹来
我们爱你
所以我们渴望你
哦 你来了 你真的来了
不是因为你爱我们
而你仅仅是路过此地
碰巧的?

Naifaru

A little boy held a bird in his hand
Walking along a way by the seaside
Three girls from the other side passed
They came from a far and alien land

The boy turned around
Quietly stepping to the girls
The girls saw him and then stopped
He gave his bird to one of the girls

The girls became excited
What a flamboyant bird!
It was a beautiful parrot
with emerald feathers

The girl opened her right hand
A tiny square for the bird to stand
The girls smiled, giggled, so glad
The boy naively blinked his eyes

那依法鲁

一个小男孩手里捧着一只鸟儿
沿着海边走来
三个女孩迎面走过去
她们来自很远的异乡

男孩转过身
轻悄悄地走近女孩
女孩看到他就停下了脚步
他把他的鸟儿给了其中一个女孩

女孩兴奋不已
多艳的一只鸟儿啊!
是一只漂亮的鹦鹉
羽毛翠绿

女孩张开她的右手
给了小鸟儿一个小小的广场
女孩笑，咯咯笑，好高兴
男孩天真地眨着眼睛

His eyes looked pure as diamond
He wore a white fine cotton shirt
No speaking as he didn't understand
Their language, new and different

His bird stood peacefully on the girl's hand
The girl held it as if she'd met an old friend
She burst with her first sentence in the end
I love you, O – I love it, so exotic a bird!

The girl put the bird carefully on her head
She formed a shape of heart with her hands
The boy understood so he innocently smiled
All was understood, more than any words

他的眼睛看上去纯如宝石
他穿一件纯棉的白衬衣
一言未语，因为他不懂
她们的话，新奇而不同

他的鸟儿乖乖地站在女孩的手掌中
女孩捧着它好似遇见了一位老朋友
终于她迸出一句话
我好爱你啊——我爱它，奇异的鸟儿！

女孩小心翼翼地将鸟儿放在了自己的头上
她用双手做了一个心形
男孩懂了，于是他纯真地笑了
一切都懂，胜过任何一个语言

Good

Good morning, my little angel!
Open your eyes and lift up your head
Old goose begins singing to her kids
Down along the river through the thistle

好的

早上好，我的小天使！
睁开你的眼，抬起头
老鹅已开始对她的孩儿唱歌了
沿着河水穿行于水中的蓟花

Shooting Star

Shooting star is the fastest song in the sky
I can't hold on to it, yet
I shot its flashing light above the stars

流星

流星是天上最快的歌
我抓不住它的旋律
却摄住了它在群星之上闪过的那一道光

Autumn Mood

Leaves are silently falling
A sea of butterfly rippling

How I want to lie down
on the sea of autumn

Recalling the dry land
I've ever walked through, and

Those who cannot be forgotten
as well the fine scenery in my mind

Memorizing the persons I loved, and
those to whom I haven't said thanks

Finally let me hold the last marigold
Falling into my nearly faded dream

秋天的心情

树叶悄然落下
蝴蝶之海荡漾

我多么想躺下来
在秋天的海洋上

回忆我曾经走过
陆地，和

那些不能被遗忘的人
以及我心存的美好景色

记住我爱的人，和
那些我还没有对他们说谢谢的人

最后让我抱着最后的金盏花
坠入我几乎褪色的梦

Existence

two goldfish
exchanged their whispers
then began chasing
the newly–arrived fish

the new fish, in fear
fleeing in the water
nowhere to escape
where is safer

even in a small pool
the things to care
perhaps, not only for survival
but also for struggle

存在

两条鱼
在交头接耳
然后，开始追逐
新来的鱼

新来的鱼，很害怕
在水中逃窜
无处可逃
哪里更安全啊？

即使在一个小小的池塘中
需要小心的事情
或许不仅仅是生存
而还有挣扎

When I get to know you

I know your heart
Gentle like floret
Want to talk to you
Your lips closed tight
Deep eyes, tender flow
What do I expect?
Young melilot
Bonny as morning light
Day to day open, so quiet
On a drifting wide-brim hat

当我认识你

我知道你的心
温柔恰似小花
想和你说话
你的唇紧闭
深情的眼睛，含情脉脉
我在期待什么？
年轻的黄香草木樨
快活得像晨光
每天静悄悄地开放
在一个漂泊的宽檐帽上

Moonflower

Your short bloom
Revived from last night's gloom

Before the frosts come
I go out of my bedroom

In the morning hour
You are what I mostly want to hear

From your forbearing face
I read your hidden phrase

I may lower my body or bend down
But sure not to hurt your fragile chin

You open a tiny trumpet to sky
You spit out a sigh of relief – Ah, my light

Short of amazing beauty, yet to shine
Night is a long process into a shine

In worldly eyes you are something just feeble
But to me, you in subtle spirit even though small

夕颜

你短暂的绽放
是从昨晚的忧伤中苏醒过来的

在霜冻到来之前
我走出我的睡房

在早晨的时光里
你是我最想听到的

从你和蔼的脸上
我读到了你隐藏的短句

我或许会降低我的身体或弯下身
但我一定不会伤到你脆弱的下巴

你对着天空打开了一个小喇叭
你吐出一声宽慰的叹息——啊，我的光

你没有惊人的美丽，却闪耀
夜要经过一个漫长的过程进入光芒

世俗眼里，你是弱不禁风的
但依我看，你虽小，却暗含勇气

A Foreigner in the Midland

He inlayed the broken porcelains into the clay wall
A withered heart stood up in the art of his longing
Afternoon sunlight reflected on the eagle's eyeball
He inlayed the broken porcelains into the clay wall
He laughed out loud it wasn't only left a sand bowl！
Beauty of the colored glaze was sowed for shining

He inlayed the broken porcelains into the clay wall
A withered heart stood up in the art of his longing

一个外国人在中原

他把破碎的陶瓷镶嵌到泥土墙里
一颗凋零的心在他渴望的艺术中站立起来
午后的阳光映在鹰的眼球上
他把破碎的陶瓷镶嵌到泥土墙里
他爽朗笑出来，这不仅仅只留下一枚砂碗啊！
他播种的五颜六色的琉璃美在闪烁

他把破碎的陶瓷镶嵌到泥土墙里
一颗凋零的心在他渴望的艺术中站立起来

Good Friends

One day, you became famous
You ran to tell me excitedly, hey
I am Eileen Chang, It's me!
O dear, I said, no wonder I am Yan Ying!

Then you changed to wear a red chi-pao
I chose to put on a white evening dress
You tied a white rose on your hair
I, put a red rose on my hair

We sipped the late autumn twilight
Under a hibiscus tree drunk into dream

好朋友

有一天，你出名了
你跑来告诉我，嘿
我是张爱玲，是我！
哦，亲爱的，我说，难怪我是炎缨！

然后你换了一件红色的旗袍
而我选择了一件白色的晚礼服
你在你的头发上系上了一朵白玫瑰
我，把一朵红玫瑰戴在我的头发上

我们啜着着深秋的暮光
在芙蓉树下醉成梦

Morning Dews

How dainty the clear morning dews！
The errant bee flies to find the hostess
No more sense of alienate petals burst forth
"Come to taste my crystal–dappled droplets!"

晨露

多么美味而清莹的晨露!
游侠般的蜜蜂飞来找到了女主人
不再感到疏远 花瓣绽放
“来尝尝我的水晶花滴吧!”

My Voice

Cicada hides in the tree
Chirping his bright songs to the summer

I hide in the night
Twittering my soundless heart to the moon …

我的声音

知了藏在树上
对着夏天唱着他清亮的歌

我躲在夜里
对着月亮呢喃着我默默的心

Holly Valley

O see, the sunny light climbs the leaves
The leaves climb the wisterias
The wisterias climb the feathery hat
The feather hat climbs the wings of delight
The wings of delight climb the deep valley
The deep valley is in the scent of rosemary
O see, please, when spring truly comes
I'll love to meet a girl spirited called Holly
She is over there turning like a butterfly
I want to put a garland on hair of the cutie
On tiptoe she stands afar like a little ballerina
O, soothing wind climbs her garland with aroma!

冬青谷

哦，看哪！阳光爬上了树叶
树叶爬上了紫藤
紫藤爬上了带有羽毛的帽子
羽毛帽爬上了欢喜的羽翼
欢喜的羽翼爬上了深深的山谷
深谷沉浸在迷迭香的清香中
哦，请看哪！春天真的来了
我多想遇见一位叫冬青的女孩
她就在那边像蝴蝶一样旋转着
我想在这个小可爱的头上放一个小花环
她正在远处踮起芭蕾脚尖
哦，舒缓的风爬上她那带着香味的小花环

Old Postcard

a book café
by roadside
named Smallage
just on last sale

discounted postcards
one yuan for one piece
I was attracted
and walked inside

the postcards
put on the gallows
I began to select
my favorite

an old man jumped
into my eyes
with a newspaper
in hand

老明信片

一个名为“野芹”的
书吧
在打折季
一元钱一张明信片

我走进去
看到黑白色调的明信片
放在木架上
我开始挑选我中意的

一个老人
进入我眼帘
他的手上
拿着一张报纸

聚精会神地读
他戴着一顶鸭舌帽
鸭舌帽带我回到
四十年代的电影

he read attentively
he wore a peaked cap
the cap took me back
to the movies in 1940s

nostalgic scene
nostalgic colour
nostalgic person
nostalgic picture

now all on sale
who likes the old time?
who likes an old postcard?
who still sends a postcard?

who else comes to buy an old time
I am here to hold the old time
even though I have no idea about
where to post it ……

怀旧的场景
怀旧的颜色
怀旧的人
怀旧的画面

都被打折了
还有谁喜欢老时光
谁喜欢老明信片
谁还寄明信片?

谁还会来买老时光
我在这里握着老时光
尽管我还没有主意
该寄给谁

Grammar

I cannot be a good poet
I have a problem with grammar
I need to be corrected
One day I said to you

But you said
Don't worry, my friend
Poetry does not have to follow the rules of grammar
A heart of a poet cannot be proofread

Cannot be edited
That is a poet's heart

语法

我不能成为一名好诗人
我有语法问题
我需要修正
有一天 我对你说

而你说
不要担心 我的朋友
诗歌不需要跟随语法规则
诗人的心是不能被校对的

不能被编辑
那是诗人的心

Minnesota

Your given name is mingni suda
In my native tongue I say it like this

The first letter is a bright spring ray
I love this beautiful girlish name

Every time I come to call this name
I feel droplets of soda moisten my lips

You are so luscious—O mingni suda
When I think of you, I taste your sweetness

明尼苏达

你的名字是明尼苏达
在我的母语里我这样念出来

第一个字符是明媚的阳光
我爱这美丽的少女般的名字

每次我念出这个名字
我感觉苏打水滋润我的唇

你是如此甜美——哦 明尼苏达
当我想你的时候 我尝到你的甜蜜

Peacock

A peacock comes to the silent river
Looking at himself in the big mirror

Ah, there's a piece of brocade clothes in the mirror
How pretty! Then he plunges into the mirror

He tries to put on the rainbow dress in the water
The river runs to hold him tight, hey, you, dear! –

Have you never seen yourself outside my mirror?
You've put your amazing wings on me, swim ashore!

孔雀

一只孔雀来到静静的河边
在一个硕大的镜子里看到了自己

啊，镜子里有一块织锦缎啊
多漂亮！然后他扑到镜子里

他试图穿上这件水中的彩虹衣裳
河水跑过来紧紧抱住他，嘿，你，亲爱的——

你从来没有在我的镜子之外看到过你自己吗？
你已经把你那奇异的羽翼披在了我的身上，游上岸吧！

Omen

Thirty three centigrade
In the morning, a hot day

He shouted down the street
Mulberry, sweet mulberry!

The street was indifferent
No one stopped for his fruit

I, as a passerby, passed away
But I picked a green apple

From my summer orchard
Back to my eastern balcony

Waiting for a magpie
to come by

预兆

三十三摄氏度
晨，炎热的一天

他沿街叫喊着
桑葚，甜桑葚喽！

街道清冷
没有人为他的桑葚停下来

我，一个过路人，走了过去
但我却摘了一枚青苹果

从我的夏日果园
我回到我的东部阳台

等待一只喜鹊
飞来

Golden Bridge

TV went on
Music arose
He and an old song
Touched my heart
"I lay me down
like a bridge
over the troubled water"
Couldn't help thinking of you
A bridge, over a rainy heaven
Lying between the clouds

金桥

电视在播放
音乐响起
他和一首老歌
触动了我的心
“我躺下来
像一座桥
横跨在忧郁河上”
我不禁想起了你
一座桥，跨越雨中的天堂
横跨在云与云之间

The Arrested

He says
Chill pill
Chill pill
So I take
My chill pill

Be patient
Wait, wind
Stop, then
Get to
Catch it

被捕

他说
冷静
冷静
所以我吃了
我的冷药丸

耐心点儿
等待，风
停止，然后
去
逮住它

Still Life

Vernal light soft
Lilac scent soft
I look for your tender fingers
Once combing my pigtails

Mirror of the year mirrors
A couple of new faces
On my windowsill
An inkstone looks like a tiny hill

Out of the windowsill
Silvery yarn floated on a far hill
What going into my eyes
Is a painting of still life

静物画

春光柔柔
丁香花柔柔
我在寻找你温柔的手
曾经给我梳过马尾头

时光的镜子闪亮
映出许多新面孔
在我的窗台上
一方砚台看上去是我的迷你小山

窗外
银色的纱漂在远山顶上
进入我眼帘的
是一幅静物画

Jade Flute

Sky is laying the mushroom seed
on the roof of his wooden cabin
Leaning against a magnolia tree
I intently stare at a wonder of shine
Find him behind a noiseless lily pond
O, a greenish flute in hands, playing
Ballade through his fingers so mild
The angelic air around, lingering long
Convey a tranquil note to heaven
The grace of serenity eases my mind

玉笛

天空正在铺设着蘑菇种子
在他的木屋的屋顶上
我靠着一棵木兰树
专注地盯着一个闪耀的奇迹
我发现他在寂静的睡莲池
哦，手上还拿着一个绿色的长笛在吹奏
牧歌流过他的手指 那么温和
天籁般的空气萦绕，挥之不去
向天堂传达一个宁静的音符
宁静中的优雅缓解了我的心

Sing My Song

Sing my song
Summer gives me a garment?
Don't moan
Just to sing
Winter's frostbite
Will be gone
Sing the song!
My heart
Longing for what?
There is no sigh
like the little owls
in my back garden
There is no complaint
like the silent eyes
Bearing my heavy night
There is no pain
Only the song
like a lark – landing
on my wounds

我唱我的歌

唱我的歌
夏天会给我一件衣裳吗?
不要呻吟
只唱歌
冬天的冻疮
就要消失
唱歌吧!
我的心
期待什么呢?
没有叹息
就像一个小猫头鹰
在我的后花园
没有抱怨
就像沉默的眼睛
承受了我沉重的夜
没有痛苦
只唱歌
像百灵鸟——降落在
我的伤口

Osmanthus

The window opened to the bright moon
Sweet scented osmanthus nodded to the wind
The wind outside curiously asked –
Why the osmanthus flowered in winter
Osmanthus did not give an answer
Lifting up brows, beaming on the moon
Fragrant air spread as if returning to August
Turning back, the wind, caught by the deep scent

桂花

窗户朝着明亮的月亮敞开
桂花向风点了点头
窗外的风好奇地问——
为什么桂花会在冬天绽放
桂花没有回答
她扬起眉毛，对着月亮面露喜色
芬芳的空气蔓延 仿佛回到了八月
风，掉过头来，被幽幽香味捕获

One Poem Is Too Short

You come to meet me once a year, yourself
Waiting for me to present you a poem
A poem is too short, only one poem –
What I want to say to you is not enough

I love to give you poetry, emotion and my heart
The only chance I cherish is like a dream
The cold rain is always falling when you come
The rainy season's rain is a heavenly gift

Well, I'm not afraid of the cold rain, it's alright
In my poem, there are rainbow, eaves and magpies
But you only come to meet me once a year
How I want to give you all my feelings with no tears

A poem is too short, only one poem –
What I want to say to you is not enough

一首诗太短

你每年只来见我一次，你
等着我献给你一首诗
一首诗太短 仅仅一首——
我想对你说的说不尽

我要给你诗歌、深情和我的心
我珍爱的仅有的机会就像一个梦
你来的时候 阴冷的雨总是降临
雨季的雨是天堂的礼物吧

好吧 我不怕凄雨 这样挺好
我的诗里 有彩虹 有屋檐 有喜鹊
可是你每年只来看我一次
我多想给你我全部的感受而不含眼泪

一首诗太短 仅一首诗——
我想对你说的说不尽

30 June

The early morning fresh rain
Gentle like blues
Dance away the grey dawn
Dance away the silence

The soft drizzle
Falling on my chin
Dancing into my eyes
Wetting my memories

I walk in the lightsome rain
Arms open to hug the good rain
The gift you send from heaven
I forget your absence on 30 June

六月三十日

早晨新鲜的雨
柔曼得像蓝调
舞动着驱除了灰色的黎明
驱除了沉寂

轻柔的细雨
落在我的下巴上
舞进我的眼睛
打湿我的记忆

我走在绵绵雨中
张开手臂拥抱这场妙雨
这是你从天堂给的礼物啊
我忘了你在六月三十日的缺席

Waiting for a Heart Back to Spring

Turn round
Ready to leave?
Lonely figure
Like a trunk of oak
Stand alone
on the moor
Turn round
Final decision?
Time to flee?
February in the air
Bring a new pioneer
Renewing the foliage
Reanimate the land
from hibernation
If now going away
A stale colour
Boringly attached
Like a winter cloud
Pale, grey, no vigor
Read the eyes

等待一颗心回到春天

转身
准备好了离开吗？
孤独的身影
好像橡树干
独自站立
在沼泽地上
转身
最后的决定？
逃离的时间？
二月的空气
从冬眠的世界
带来一个新的先锋
更新的叶子
复活的土地
如果现在要离开
只能带着陈旧的颜色
乏味的附属
像一块冬天的云
苍白的，灰暗的，没有活力
读你的眼睛

Reveal a state of mood

What a cool face!

Turn back, turn

Look ahead, ahead

This season

Soon be warmed

This shore

Soon be fair

透露了心情
多么酷的脸！
转回来，转
向前看，向前看
这个季节
很快就被捂暖
此岸
很快就会晴朗

Simple

There is an old woman
Crouching at a corner
Under a red brick wall
Reading a picture–book

Someone passing by
Laugh at her a bit silly
Someone seeing her
Laugh at her too childish

I stop by, looking at her
Her carefree smile on her lips
Telling me how happy she is
Why not, squat down next to her

Lean on the wall and close my eyes
In the Sept mild sun, feel the breeze
Brushing lightly on my face
Murmuring a word softly, softly to me

单纯

有一个老妇人
蜷缩在一个角落里
在一个红色的砖墙下面
读一本小人儿书

有人路过这里
笑她有点儿傻
有人看见她
嘲笑她太幼稚

我停下来，看着她
她那泛起无忧无虑笑意的嘴唇
告诉我她是多么的快乐
为什么不呢，蹲在她旁边？

靠在墙上，我闭上了眼睛
在九月和煦的阳光里，感觉习习微风
轻轻拂面
呢喃着，轻轻地，轻轻地对我

Temple

I open my window
You, on my opposite side
Also open your window

My lips slightly open
Tasty like chardonnay
Cherries climb the treetops

The visitor is not you
A day in early June
Wrapped in rice dumpling

Straw rain cape is olive green
Cicadas not yet wake up
A lifelike statue set on a roof
Which ditty comes first from afar?

寺庙

我打开窗
你，在我的对面
也敞开你的窗

我的嘴唇微微张开
美味的似夏顿埃酒
樱桃爬上树梢

到访的人不是你
那一天是六月初
被包在粽子里

蓑衣是橄榄绿
蝉还没有醒来
一座栩栩如生的雕像置于屋顶
哪一首小调最先从远方而至

You Cried Last Night

You cried last night
I caressed my moonlight
as if I had touched a drizzling night

You cried last night
I stood at my balcony
and upraised a bunch of peony

You cried last night
I was in the deep night
and accompanied you to dawning light

昨晚你哭了

昨晚你哭了
我抚摸我的月光
仿佛抚摸绵绵细雨的夜

昨晚你哭了
我站在我的阳台
举起一束牡丹花

昨晚你哭了
我就在深夜里
陪你到曙光升起

Enschede

You were a brown colored notebook
Wrapped by the old bark of a forest
I walked 9000 kilometers to hold you
I turned to your first page with my zest

On this page jumped out a windmill
I rode on a knight's humor as natives
Then I turned to the second page, so
I came across a line of footprints of the elk

Turning over the page again
I saw your sad left ear
I heard a dolorous whisper
Coming from a field of poppies

Purple petals fell, a groan of pains fell
The windmill turning to heaven
Played a song of Coldplay so lyrical
by my right ear, lingering, lingering

恩斯赫德

你是一本棕色的笔记本
被森林的老树皮包裹
我走了九千公里来捧起你
我满怀热情翻到你的第一页

这一页 跳出一个大风轮
我就像本土人乘着一个骑士的幽默
然后我翻到第二页 于是
我遇见了一行麋鹿的脚印

一页一页地翻下去
我看见你忧伤的左耳
我听到了一串伤心的耳语
来自罂粟的田野

紫色的花瓣落下 痛苦的呻吟落下
风轮转向天堂
奏起一首酷玩的抒情曲
在我的右耳边萦绕 萦绕

I Need the Sun

Scenery is boundless
Poetry is infinite
I want to have the brilliant sun
to sparkle on my wounded back
To put out the evil fire
in the depth of my soul

我需要太阳

风景是无边的
诗意是无限的
我想拥有璀璨的阳光
喷射在我受损的背脊上
扑灭我灵魂深处的
邪恶之火

Chance

You have a lot of chances
And I don't have

You meet a lot of stunning fishes
I just catch some seaweed

You say we all have chances
Keep your chin up

If your chance is the duckweed
Mine are the stars beyond the clouds

机会

你有好多机会
而我没有

你遇见了许多惊奇的鱼
我只是抓到了一些海藻

你说 我们都有机会
不要泄气

假如你的机会是浮萍
我的就是云边的星星

Gift

A picture painted inside of an eggshell
A court lady was chasing two butterflies

A picture painted on a square–shaped bark
A pair of lovers danced a dance for a king

We used the third language saying to each other
Hey, it's for you – Here you are!

We took these handcrafted things as treasure
After that we wrote to each other via a letter

The painted bark was now hung on my wall —
The painted eggshell was placed on your bookshelf

礼物

蛋壳内画着一幅画
一个宫女在追逐两只蝴蝶

树皮上画有一幅画
一对情侣在为一个国王跳舞

我们用第三种语言对彼此说
嘿，给你的 拿着！

我们把这些手工制作的东西当宝
从此以后，我们互相通信

树皮画现在挂在我的墙上——
内壁画蛋壳放在你的书架上

When You Say I am an Angel

Angel has no faults
But I have faults
Angle loves everyone
I only love a few
Angel has no trouble
I make trouble
Angel rises in heaven
I fall on earth
Angel is a beauty of eternal
I am a little potato
When you say I am an angel
I feel ashamed coz I am too small

当你说我是安琪儿

安琪儿没有瑕疵
而我有瑕疵
安琪儿爱每个人
而我只爱几个
安琪儿没有麻烦
而我有麻烦
安琪儿在天堂上升
而我落在地上
安琪儿是永恒的美人
而我是一个小土豆儿
当你说我是安琪儿
我感到羞愧 因为我太渺小

Softly, Softly

Softly, someone knocks at the door
No need to ask who it is
I am familiar with the way it comes

Softly, someone hums a lyrical song
Do not ask who is singing this song
I know the way she does for release

Softly, someone turns away from the shore
Do not ask why he leaves the world behind
I understand the reason for his fated end

Softly, something appears and disappears
Softly, someone comes and then gone …
That is the way of the world, for sure

轻轻地，轻轻地

轻轻地，有人敲门
无需问是谁
我熟悉它来的方式

轻轻地，有人哼着一首抒情的歌
不要问是谁在唱这首歌
我知道她释放的方式

轻轻地，有人转身离开岸边
不要问他为什么把世界抛在身后
我理解他的命运终结的原因

轻轻地，有些事出现 有些事消失
轻轻地，有人来了，然后走了……
无疑，这就是世界的方式

She'd Never Lost Her Voice

My mother acted a modern drama in my dream
Her voice was sounding like the wind chime
I stood under a black–and–white ginkgo tree
Listening to her voice so vivid by my ears
Distant spotlight flashed above the tree but dim
I couldn't see her face though I heard her voice
Clearly I heard her recite the drama lines
Moonlight was flowing like a silvery waterfall
Her voice was what I wanted to grasp as a miracle
I lived in my dream to see she'd never lost her voice
Who would love to hide in a dream to catch a voice?
I would! – collect my mother's real voice in my dream

她从未失去过她的声音

我母亲在我的梦里出演了一场话剧
她的声音听起来好似风铃
我站在一棵黑白色的银杏树下
听着她如此生动的声音回响在我的耳畔
遥远的聚光灯在树的上方闪烁 却昏暗
看不到她的脸 尽管我听见了她的声音
我清晰地听到她朗诵台词
月光像一道银色的瀑布流淌下来
她的声音是我想要抓住的奇迹
我住在我的梦里清醒地知道她永远都不会失去她的声音
谁会喜欢躲在一个梦里只为抓住一个声音?
我会!—— 我会在我的梦里收集我母亲的真切声音

Fishing

The fishing man is old
Sitting by the lakeside
in a daze or fishing
Whose luck is good?

The result is not seen
Fish is on the hook
He yet to find the luck
The man in a trance

Gazing at the quiet lake
He thought of something
While fishing, fishing
is a kind of camouflage

Luck may be changed
What ought to come
Yet to come
Nothing comes, heart tamed

垂钓

渔夫老了
坐在岸边
发呆 抑或捕鱼
谁的运气好呢?

结果却看不见
鱼在钩上
他还没有找到运气
恍惚中的男人

凝视着平静的湖水
他想着一些心事
看似钓鱼，钓鱼
恰是一种伪装

运气可能会改变
应该来的，
尚未到来
没什么可来 心被驯服

Poet

You are a spiritual animal
Prophetic or unpredictable
From your cryptic looks of eyes
I see the sea, magma and moonrise

诗人

你是灵性的动物
先知的或不可预知的
从你神秘的眼神中
我看到海、岩浆和月亮

Mottled Graffiti

Going to the Thames River
Passing through you——
Mottled graffiti on the wall
Dazzle my curious eyes
Fail to say out your name
You Mighty Excellence King
Millennium Bridge on the river
Already outstrip your splendor
Mysterious hues cover your past glory
Yet, when you become a painting
Wheel of the faded time rolls back
Memories aroused by your old charm
Yesterday once more you looked handsome
No one competed – you were handsome···

斑驳的涂鸦

去泰晤士河
经过了你——
墙上斑驳的涂鸦
令我好奇的眼睛眼花缭乱
说不出你的名字
您伟大的卓越之王
千禧桥跨越在河上
早已超越了你的辉煌
神秘的色彩掩盖了你昔日的荣光
然而，当你成为一幅画
失去的光轮翻滚回来
记忆被你古老的魅力激起
昨日从现 你看起来很帅
没人能比——你曾经很帅 ……

Air Route

I don't know from what time
Here, become the new route
Planes sweep through the roofs
Passing by every twenty minutes
How many twenty minutes in a day?
How many times for going away?
To the south, north, east or west
To a familiar domain or strange world
Drag a long white ribbon behind
Slide into the clouds until unseen
Higher and farther, with a heart
of looking back, or to forget ···

航线

我不知道从什么时候开始
这里成为了新航线
飞机掠过屋顶
每二十分钟过往一次
一天当中有多少个二十分钟？
多少次离去？
去东南西北
去熟悉的疆域或陌生的世界
身后拖着一条白色的长丝带
滑入云端直到看不见
越来越高越远，带着一颗
回望之心，或遗忘……

One and Two

I have two
You only have one
When I have two
You already have
a window of world
You have one
But much bigger
than my two

一个和两个

我有两个
你却只有一个
当我拥有两个
你已经拥有
一扇世界之窗
你有一个
却比我的两个
大了很多

In the Field of Reed

Autumn breeze blows your scarf
Reeds unaware of the direction, swing
Red berries turn crimson
Whose dimples are more crimson ?
The fall more or less looks grief
Your shadow flashes, swept off by autumn

在芦苇地

秋风吹着你的围巾
芦苇不知道方向，摇摆
红色的浆果变得深红
谁的笑靥看起来更深红?
秋天或多或少有些悲伤
你的影子一闪，被秋天掠去

Minor in the North

Falling raindrops
Harmonious notes

dou rai mi fa sou …
sou fa mi rai dou …

I hear the autumn buds
Jump out of my eaves

Slide down the roof
Brave enough

Touches on my eyelid
The ditty, subtle cold

北方小调

雨滴落下
和谐的音符

抖 莱 咪 发 嗖
嗖 发 咪 莱 抖

我听见秋天的蓓蕾
跳出我的瓦檐

从屋顶上滑下来
足够勇敢

触到我的眼帘
这支小曲，微微凉意

Chocolate Balls

I see a vast field of brown colored flowers
in a countryside, like small chocolate balls

This is a clear sign of the mid–autumn festival
Sweet with a little bitter taste – autumn's gifts

Savoury and mellow, fall on the earth of grass
Fall on my memory of yesterday, fall into soil

I bend down to watch the floral chocolate balls
Softly colliding each other in the wind, so gentle

巧克力球

我看到一片田地开满棕色的花朵
在乡村，花朵就像小巧克力球

这分明是中秋节的迹象
甜甜的味道带点苦味——秋天的礼物

香醇可意，落在草地上
落入我昔日的记忆，落进泥土

我弯下身看着巧克力小花球
在风中轻轻碰撞，如此温柔

The Falling Beauty

What will you think of
when you feel sad?
withered petals
cold rains, and
wild hawthorns
that drop onto the ground
but no one picks them up
on the forgotten slope

Why always connecting in mind
the faded scene, like autumn
actually, autumn's sorrows
might not be so decadent or bad
the leaves spin into your arms
then it reminds you of butterflies
yes, dancing butterflies
the last dance is the butterfly!

飘逝的美丽

当你感到忧伤的时候
你会想到什么？
枯萎的花朵
冰冷的雨，还是
野山楂
落在被人遗忘的
斜坡
没人捡起

为什么总是联想到
褪色的景象，就像秋天
实际上，秋天的悲伤
或许并不那么颓废和糟糕
叶子炫舞到你的怀里
然后你想起了蝴蝶
是的，跳舞的蝴蝶
最后的舞蹈就是蝴蝶！

Old Jinling

Rusty doorsills
Narrow alleys
Stone houses
Dusty windows
Salted Duck
Stinky tofu
Lush plane trees
Sky's screen
Riverstones
Confucius Temple
Xuanwu Lake
Ying Fu Street
Plum blossoms
Climbed into Qinhuai River
I sat on the riverbank
Seeing him come by
Grandpa, Grandpa!
I cried out in a hoarse voice
He didn't look back
Wasn't he my grandpa …?

古老金陵

生锈的门槛
狭窄的巷子
石头房
落灰的窗
咸水鸭
臭豆腐
葱郁的树
天空的屏
雨花石
夫子庙
玄武湖
鹰福街
梅花丛
爬进秦淮河
我坐在河岸
看着他经过
爷爷，爷爷
我用沙哑的声音喊
他没有回头
他不是我爷爷吗？

Flow

Small river
Soft and slender
No fisherman
No shore
I put my paper moon
in the water
Drift, drift farther
to an end of unseen

流

小小的河
轻缓而细长
没有渔夫
没有岸
我把我的纸月亮
放进水里
飘啊飘，飘到更远处
飘到一个看不见的尽头

My Eternal Sky

I say, I am afraid
My sky shifts away
My golden star dies away

You say, hey, little bud
Your sky won't move away
If you look into my eyes

The light of my eyes
Blink for you never lose
Gaze at me — sky returns

我永恒的天空

我说，我怕
我的天空会移走
我那颗金星会消失

你说，嘿，小花蕾
你的天空不会移开
如果你看着我的眼睛

我眼里的光
对你闪烁呢 永不遗失
凝望我——天空回来了

Translated Poems©

The Banyan Tree

by Syed Zaigham Shafiq Jaffery©, Architect, Poet, Pakistan

Fleeting shadows
of the flame
singe the farthest corners
of the heart

Blood in the tears
etches tales untold
and the eyes melt
in the heat of the wait

She was here, I know
she passed this way
perfumes of her body
linger in the air

I inhale her fragrance
deep inside me
she now resides

翻译诗作三首

榕树

作品原创：Syed Zaigham Shafiq Jaffery©, 巴基斯坦建筑师、诗人

火焰掠过的
影子
燎到我心灵深处
最远的角落

赤红的泪
蚀刻在从未讲过的故事里
眼睛
融化在等待的灼热里

我知道，她就在这里
她经过这条路
身上的香味
飘在空气中 香满径

我深深吸吮
这奇香
她就驻在我心里

And I wait
for the moon
to re-appear
from behind
the dark clouds
of doubt

I will sit here and wait
til' I grow
into a banyan tree
I will shade here
as she rests
under me
and reaches
a conclusion
My love is pure
It will grow

I think
I know …

我等待
月亮
在我身后
重现
拨开
黑暗的疑云

我就坐在这里等待
直到我长成
一颗榕树
当她栖息在这里
我会在这儿遮阴
在我的绿荫下
怡享安然
度过此生

我的爱如此纯洁
久久地滋长、蔓延

我思念
我心知

Tr. Cigeng Zhang
翻译：张次庚

The Woman in Red.

by Omar Eldamsheety©， Engineer, Poet, Egypt

That lovely woman in red,
with a little girl's mind,
reads 'Little Red Riding Hood',
and hears wolves sound.

By mistake, she smiled to me,
so, I smiled and said Hello,
her face changed suddenly,
and shouted, you are a wolf, go.

What did I do to frighten her?
I live in peace, I'm so good.
What is the matter with her? I wonder.
She reads 'Little Red Riding Hood'.

穿红衣的女人

作品原创：Omar Eldamsheety©, 埃及工程师、诗人

那个穿红衣的女人真可爱，
她有着一颗小女孩儿般的心。
她在读“小红帽”，而且，
听到了狼的声音

不经意地，她对我笑了笑
所以，我也笑了笑，说，你好。
她的脸色突然变了，
并大声说，你是一只狼，走开。

我做了什么吓着了她?
我生活在和平中，我可是个好人。
她到底怎么了？我不知道。
她读着“小红帽”。

Tr. Cigeng Zhang
翻译：张次庚

Flora Deity

©by Iain Davie, Poet, Pilot, the UK,

Flora deity
Lady rose
Nymph Khloris
Errant bee is but
Zephyr wind God
Of west wind
Tending to your fruit
Errant bee
Must stay with thee
That your sweetest bud
Shall bloom
Wave and shuddering the breeze
Wave and shuddering the breeze

芙罗拉女神

作品原创：Iain Davie©，英国诗人、飞行员

芙罗拉女神啊
玫瑰娇人
女神克罗里斯
迷途的蜜蜂
恰似西风中的
泽费风神
奔向你的花果
迷途的蜜蜂
必须和你在一起
你的繁花
花瓣突出
你最甜蜜的花蕾
将要开花
香波涟漪 震颤着微风
香波涟漪 震颤着微风

Tr. Cigeng Zhang
翻译：张次庚

Poetry makes us beautiful while we make poetry alive.

—Cigeng Zhang

诗歌令我们美丽；我们让诗歌活。

——张次庚

图书在版编目（CIP）数据

水中的胭脂：汉英对照 / 张次庚著 .—桂林：漓江出版社，2016.12
ISBN 978-7-5407-7997-9
Ⅰ .①水… Ⅱ .①张… Ⅲ .①诗集—中国—当代—汉、英 Ⅳ .① I227
中国版本图书馆 CIP 数据核字（2016）第 314233 号

水中的胭脂

作　　者：张次庚
责任编辑：谷　磊　王成成
装帧设计：黄　菲
责任监印：周　萍

出 版 人：刘迪才
出版发行：漓江出版社
社　　址：广西桂林市南环路22号
邮　　编：541002
发行电话：010-85893190　0773-2583322
传　　真：010-85890870-814　0773-2582200
邮购热线：0773-2583322
电子信箱：ljcbs@163.com　http://www.Lijiangbook.com
印　　制：北京大运河印刷有限责任公司
开　　本：710 × 960　1/32　**印　　张**：8.25　**字　　数**：22千字
版　　次：2017年1月第1版
印　　次：2017年1月第1次印刷
书　　号：ISBN 978-7-5407-7997-9
定　　价：38.00元